Two Minute Teddy Bear Tales

Ladybird

Contents

Ladybird Books Inc., Auburn, Maine 04210, U.S.A.
Published by Ladybird Books Ltd., Loughborough, Leicestershire, U.K.

Text © JOAN STIMSON 1994
Illustrations © NIGEL McMULLEN 1994
LADYBIRD and the associated pictorial device are trademarks of Ladybird Books Ltd.

*All rights reserved. No part of this publication may be reproduced,
stored in a retrieval system, or transmitted in any form or by any
means, electronic, mechanical, photocopying, recording or otherwise,
without the prior consent of the copyright owners.*

Printed in Canada

Two
Minute
Teddy Bear
Tales

by Joan Stimson

illustrated by Nigel McMullen

It Was Teddy!

Carl was a careless little boy. But he didn't like to admit it.

So, when he turned on the faucet and flooded the bathroom, he wouldn't own up. "It was Teddy!" he told his parents.

The same thing happened when Carl left his ice-cream cone on the table, and it melted into a mess.

"What a waste!" said Mom.

"What a CARELESS Teddy!" sighed Carl.

And then one day Carl accidentally hurled a ball through Mrs. Weaver's window.

"NAUGHTY Teddy!" said naughty Carl.

"I think Teddy needs to learn a thing or two," said Dad. And he went to talk to Carl's teacher.

Now Carl and Teddy had just started school. But Carl enjoyed it, and he worked hard.

"Next week," Miss Mulberry told the children, "we will be having an important visitor. And I want you all to paint a nice picture for her."

Carl painted his best picture ever. Miss Mulberry put it on the wall along with the others.

When the important visitor arrived, she was impressed. "What wonderful paintings!" she exclaimed. Then she took a closer look and pointed to Carl's. "Who painted this one?" she asked. "It's outstanding."

Carl squirmed with pride and Miss Mulberry smiled across the room. "It was Teddy!" she told the visitor.

That evening Carl took a glass of milk up to his room. But he soon came down again.

"Sorry Dad," said Carl, "I've spilled my milk and made a mess."

Mom looked amazed. "Who taught you to own up?" she asked.

Carl beamed at his parents. Then he told them, "IT WAS TEDDY!"

Another story tomorrow.

9

The Bear Who Didn't Like Hugs

"Excuse me!" muttered Panda. And he shuffled to the back of the toy shop window.

"What ARE you doing?" grumbled the other bears.

"Don't you WANT to be sold?" growled Large Brown. And he slid straight into Panda's space.

Just then, a tiny girl came bouncing along the sidewalk. She pointed to Large Brown and dragged her mom into the shop.

The shopkeeper reached carefully into the window. He scooped up Large Brown and presented him to the girl.

"OOOOOOH!" she squealed, giving him a huge hug.

"Hooray!" whispered the other bears... all except Panda.

"What's the matter?" squeaked Plump Blue. "Don't you want to go to a good home?"

Panda shook his head. "I don't like hugs!" he mumbled.

"Why on earth not?" asked the other bears. "You'll NEVER find a kind owner if you don't!"

Weeks passed, and bears came and went.

"I wish *I* could be sold!" sighed Plump Blue.

"I don't!" muttered Panda, and he settled down for a nap.

Suddenly he was woken by an excited shriek. It was a smiling girl in a blue track suit. And she was pointing straight at Panda.

"Come on, Grandpa," she cried. "Let's go into the toy shop."

Panda held his breath. The shopkeeper reached briskly into the display. SCOOP! "Here's Panda," he said. But then he scooped again. "And here's a VERY cuddly teddy bear." The shopkeeper presented the girl with Plump Blue.

Somehow they seemed made for each other. The girl couldn't stop hugging Plump Blue. And Panda heaved a sigh of relief. But he was in for a shock.

"We'll take BOTH bears!" Grandpa told the shopkeeper.

When they reached the girl's home, her mom scolded Grandpa. "Imagine buying TWO teddy bears!" she exclaimed.

"HRUMPH!" Grandpa looked sheepish. Then he explained. "The Panda's for me," he said. "He reminds me of my very first bear. And he looks like just the right bear to keep me company... in my big trailer truck."

Panda couldn't believe his ears. He couldn't wait to become a truck-driving bear. And, although he never DID get to like hugs, when Grandpa patted his shoulder each night and said, "Home at last," Panda was the happiest bear on the road.

Another story tomorrow.

Seven Sporty Bears

Monday's bear runs far and wide,
Tuesday's bear can bike and ride;

Wednesday's bear plays ball with me,
Thursday's bear can climb a tree;

Friday's bear jumps—*splash!*—in puddles,
Saturday's bear is best at cuddles;

But Sunday's bear, I'm proud to say,
Just scored a goal…
Hip, hip, HOORAY!

Turn the page for another teddy bear rhyme.

Midnight in the Park

You know the bear from Number Nine,
She likes to play at night;
DOWN the drainpipe watch her whiz,
There's not a soul in sight.

She tries a cartwheel on the grass,
She longs to stretch her paws;
Then on the swing she starts to sing,
"It's great to be outdoors!"

"Psst!" Who's that creeping up the path?
They want to try the slide!
It's Twenty-three and Seven-B—
"We couldn't stay inside."

Now Twenty-two is coming too,
And Seventeen and Four.
They're jumping off the
  jungle gym,
Then running back for more.

But suddenly a light appears,
"What's going on out there?"
A small boy cries and tries to see,
"And where's my teddy bear?"

UP the drainpipe, home they go,
Before it starts to rain.
They leave the park all still
  and dark,
But they'll be back again!

Another
story
tomorrow.

A Stitch in Time

"Cheer up, Teddy!"
began Rabbit.

"It's a beautiful, sunny
day," continued Dog.

"And you should be
HAPPY!" finished Cat.

"But I AM happy," Teddy told them.
"It's just that my mouth turns down at the
corners. And I can't do anything about it."

"Good heavens!" cried Cat. SHE had a
smile as wide as her face.

"Do you mean you were MADE that way?"
grinned Dog and Rabbit together.

Teddy nodded sadly. "No matter how
happy I feel inside," he explained,
"I always LOOK miserable. If only I had
even a small smile, I'm sure Boy would
spend more time with me."

That night, when Teddy was asleep,
Rabbit, Dog, and Cat lay awake. At last
they came up with a plan.

Next day they told Teddy what he had to do.

"Will it hurt?" he asked.

Rabbit, Dog, and Cat shook their heads. "Not much," they said.

After dinner Boy took his bath.

"Just look at this T-shirt!" cried his mom. "It's almost torn in half."

And she opened the bathroom door and threw the T-shirt across the hallway. The T-shirt landed on the sewing pile.

"NOW!" cried Rabbit, Dog, and Cat.

Teddy leaned over the edge of the top bunk. "OUCH!" He bounced onto the floor, across the hallway, and straight onto the top of the sewing pile.

When Boy woke up next morning, Teddy was propped up at the foot of his bed. Rabbit, Dog, and Cat grinned and waited.

"What are YOU smiling about?" Boy asked Teddy.

But Teddy didn't say a word. He just smiled back.

"Come on," cried Boy suddenly. He grabbed Teddy and jumped out of bed.

"It's a beautiful, sunny day. And we're going to play outside together… ALL MORNING!"

Another story tomorrow.

25

My Owner

My owner has a rumpled bed;
She sometimes won't get washed!
But I don't care if she snores or squirms,
And I don't mind getting squashed!

"Let's play a game," she sometimes cries,
And "Teddy, you begin."
But sometimes, when we play
   a game,
I WISH she'd let me win!

My owner sometimes stamps and shouts,
(She's not a pretty sight!)
But even when the grownups glare,
I'M there to hold her tight.

My owner likes to go on trips,
By boat or train or bus;
And if I didn't go with her,
I know there'd be a fuss.

Of course, we have our ups and downs,
But still we both agree—
I wouldn't change her for the world,
And she would not change me!

The end.